R. WISE

Make Hay While the Sun Shines

A Book of Proverbs

CHOSEN BY ALISON M. ABEL

Illustrated by Shirley Hughes

FABER AND FABER
London

First published in 1977
by Faber and Faber Limited
3 Queen Square London WC1
Printed in Great Britain by
Latimer Trend & Company Ltd Plymouth
All rights reserved

ISBN 0 571 11006 1

Contents

Make hay while the sun shines

Do a job when the time seems right. (If you leave it you may not get such a good opportunity again.)

Look before you leap

Be sure you know what you're letting yourself in for before you do anything drastic.

All work and no play makes Jack a dull boy

You won't do your work well if you don't rest and play too.

A stitch in time saves nine

If you put something right as soon as it goes wrong, you won't have so much trouble later.

Many hands make light work

A job is done more quickly and easily if a lot of people help.

Too many cooks spoil the broth

If too many people all try to do the same work at the same time, they can make a dreadful mess of it!

Every cloud has a silver lining

Even the worst things that happen have a good side to them.

Don't count your chickens before they're hatched

Don't plan too far ahead, and don't rely on things always turning out well for you.

The early bird catches the worm

If you want the best, then you must get there first—late-comers miss their chance.

A bird in the hand is worth two in the bush

What you have is worth more to you than something twice as valuable that you haven't got.

People who live in glass houses shouldn't throw stones

Don't criticize other people if you have the same faults yourself.

Every horse thinks his pack the heaviest

People always think that they have a harder time than anyone else.

The leopard can't change his spots

People can't change the way they are made.

Let sleeping dogs lie

Don't stir up trouble.

Once bitten, twice shy

People who have been upset or hurt once don't risk the same thing happening again.

It's no use crying for the moon

There's no point in hankering after something you know you can't have.

It's no use crying over spilt milk

Once you've made a mistake, worrying about it won't put things right.

A watched pot never boils

Things you are waiting for seem never to happen if you keep thinking about them. (Forget them, and you may be taken by surprise!)

The grass is always greener on the other side

What you haven't got always looks better than what you have.

The night is always darkest just before the dawn

Things are always at their worst just before they start to get better.

Great oaks from little acorns grow

Important things often start in a small way.

It's no use keeping a dog and barking yourself

If you ask other people to do something for you, let them get on with it and don't try to take over.

All that glitters is not gold

Not everything that looks attractive is really valuable.

Don't put all your eggs in one basket

Don't rely too much on one particular thing. (Then you won't lose everything if you are let down.)

Don't have too many irons in the fire

Don't try to do too many things at the same time.

A cat may look at a king

We all have a right to our own opinions, even about the most important people.

Pride goes before a fall

Self-important people come to grief sooner or later.

Don't change horses in mid-stream

If you've started doing something one way, don't change
your methods half-way through.

If you've made your bed you must lie on it

If you've made a mistake you must put up with the results.

Half a loaf is better than no bread

It's better to have only a little of what you need than
nothing at all.

Don't empty the baby out with the bathwater

If you're making sweeping changes, be sure you don't get rid of the good things along with the bad.

Jack of all trades is master of none

Someone who tries to do a lot of different things is unlikely to do any of them very well.

While the cat's away the mice will play

People do as they please when the person they are afraid of is out of the way.